T0418303

DOG BREEDS

ROTTWEILERS

BY KIMBERLY ZIEMANN

WWW.APEXEDITIONS.COM

Apex is distributed by North Star Editions:
sales@northstareditions.com | 888-417-0195

Produced for Apex by Red Line Editorial.

Photographs ©: Shutterstock Images, cover, 6–7, 10–11, 12, 14, 16–17, 18, 19, 20–21, 25, 29; iStockphoto, 1, 4–5, 8–9, 13, 22–23, 24, 26

Library of Congress Control Number: 2023922213

ISBN
978-1-63738-913-3 (hardcover)
978-1-63738-953-9 (paperback)
979-8-89250-050-0 (ebook pdf)
979-8-89250-011-1 (hosted ebook)

Printed in the United States of America
Mankato, MN
082024

NOTE TO PARENTS AND EDUCATORS

Apex books are designed to build literacy skills in striving readers. Exciting, high-interest content attracts and holds readers' attention. The text is carefully leveled to allow students to achieve success quickly. Additional features, such as bolded glossary words for difficult terms, help build comprehension.

TABLE OF CONTENTS

CHAPTER 1

PROTECTIVE PET

It's the middle of the night. A rottweiler sleeps on her dog bed. Suddenly, her ears perk up. She hears footsteps outside.

Dogs can hear sounds that are soft or far away.

The rottweiler runs to a window. She sees a stranger on the porch. The man is trying to open the front door. The dog barks loudly.

FAST FACT

Guard dogs watch for **threats**. They may bark or growl to alert their owners.

Rottweilers make good guard dogs. They are brave and smart.

With the right training, rottweilers can get along very well with children.

The dog's family wakes up. They see the stranger running away. They praise their dog for protecting them. She wags her tail as they pet her.

LOYAL DOGS

Rottweilers tend to be loving and **loyal** to their families. But they may not trust new people or dogs. They may bark or growl at strangers.

CHAPTER 2

WORKING DOGS

During the **Roman Empire**, soldiers used dogs to guard and **drive** cattle. Romans took over an area called Rottweil about 2,000 years ago. That area is now part of Germany.

People used rottweilers to keep herds of cattle together.

Rottweilers kept people, animals, and houses safe.

The Romans left Rottweil around 200 CE. But some of their dogs stayed. They became the rottweiler **breed**. For many years, the dogs pulled carts and drove cattle.

ROTTWEILERS REPLACED

By the mid-1800s, people began using trains or donkeys to move things. Rottweilers nearly died out. But people worked to save them. They found other work for the dogs.

Butchers often owned rottweilers. The dogs helped them take meat to markets.

COLLAR

In the 1900s, rottweilers began doing other jobs. Some were police dogs. Others helped soldiers. Rottweilers also became popular pets.

Rottweilers were police and army dogs in World War I (1914–1918). Many countries still use them.

CHAPTER 3

POWERFUL PUPS

Rottweilers are large dogs. They can weigh 80 to 135 pounds (36 to 61 kg). They can stand 27 inches (69 cm) tall at the shoulder.

Rottweilers can take three years to reach their full size.

The rottweiler is one of the strongest dog breeds.

Rottweilers were bred to pull heavy carts. They are very muscular. They also have wide heads and chests.

THE DOCKING DEBATE

People often **dock** the tails of rottweiler puppies. Short tails can help working dogs avoid getting hurt. But some people worry that docking harms the dogs. So, they leave their dogs' tails long.

In the past, dogs' tails were docked so they didn't catch on things. Today, tail docking is more about looks.

FAST FACT

Rottweilers have a thick second layer of fur. It helps them stay warm.

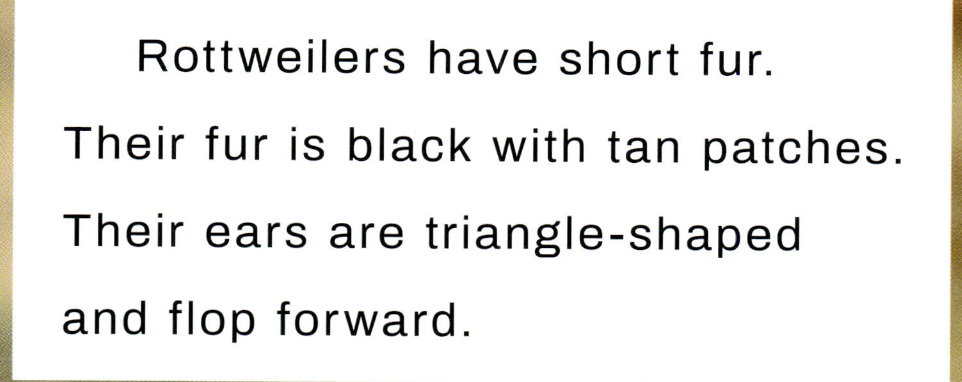

Rottweilers have short fur. Their fur is black with tan patches. Their ears are triangle-shaped and flop forward.

Rottweilers have tan patches on their faces, throats, chests, and legs.

CHAPTER 4

CARE AND TRAINING

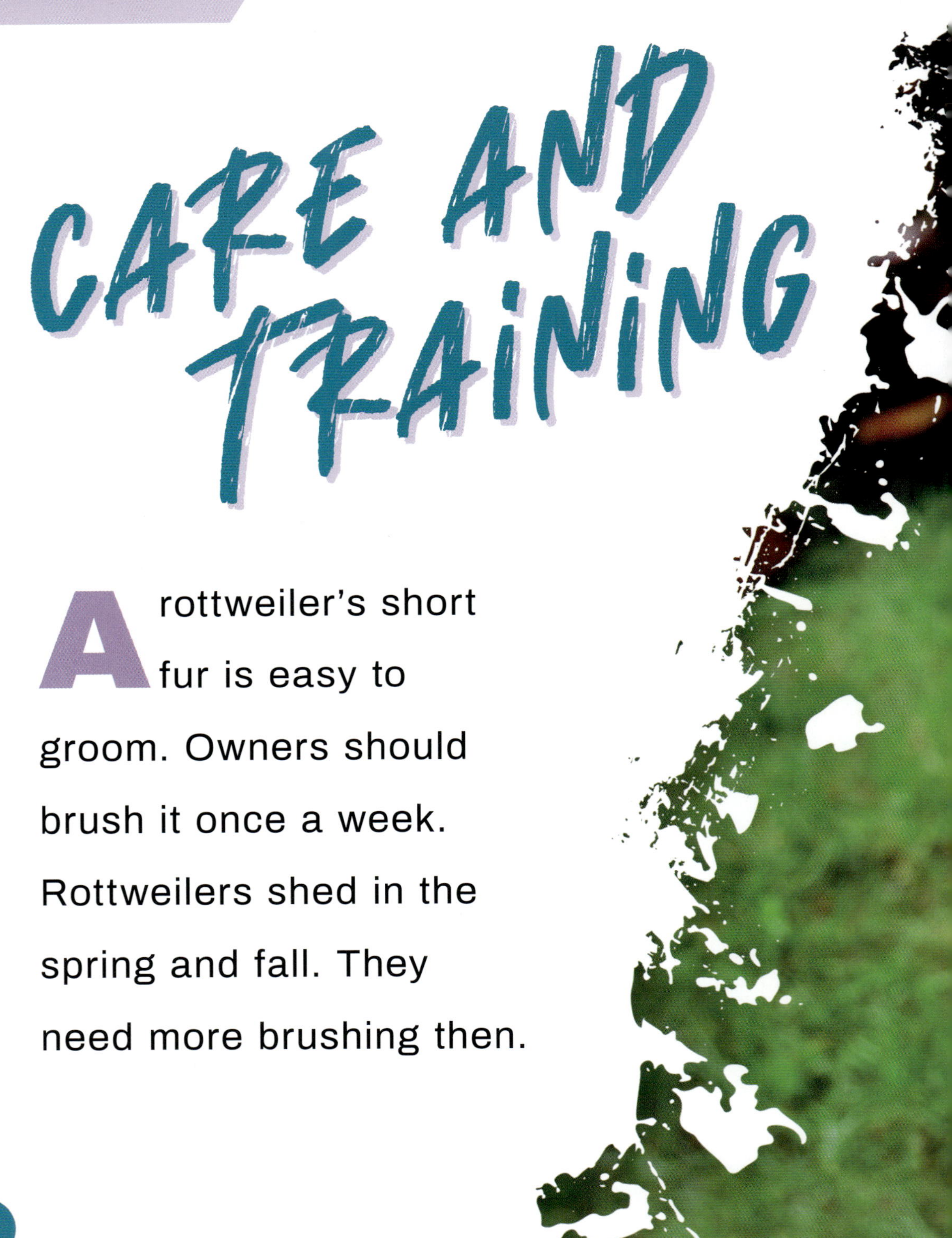

A rottweiler's short fur is easy to groom. Owners should brush it once a week. Rottweilers shed in the spring and fall. They need more brushing then.

Owners should clean rottweilers' ears regularly. Floppy ears can trap dirt.

Owners can play fetch with their rottweilers.

Rottweilers were bred to work, so they are energetic. They need exercise every day. The dogs should run or play for one to two hours.

Drinking water helps rottweilers stay cool.

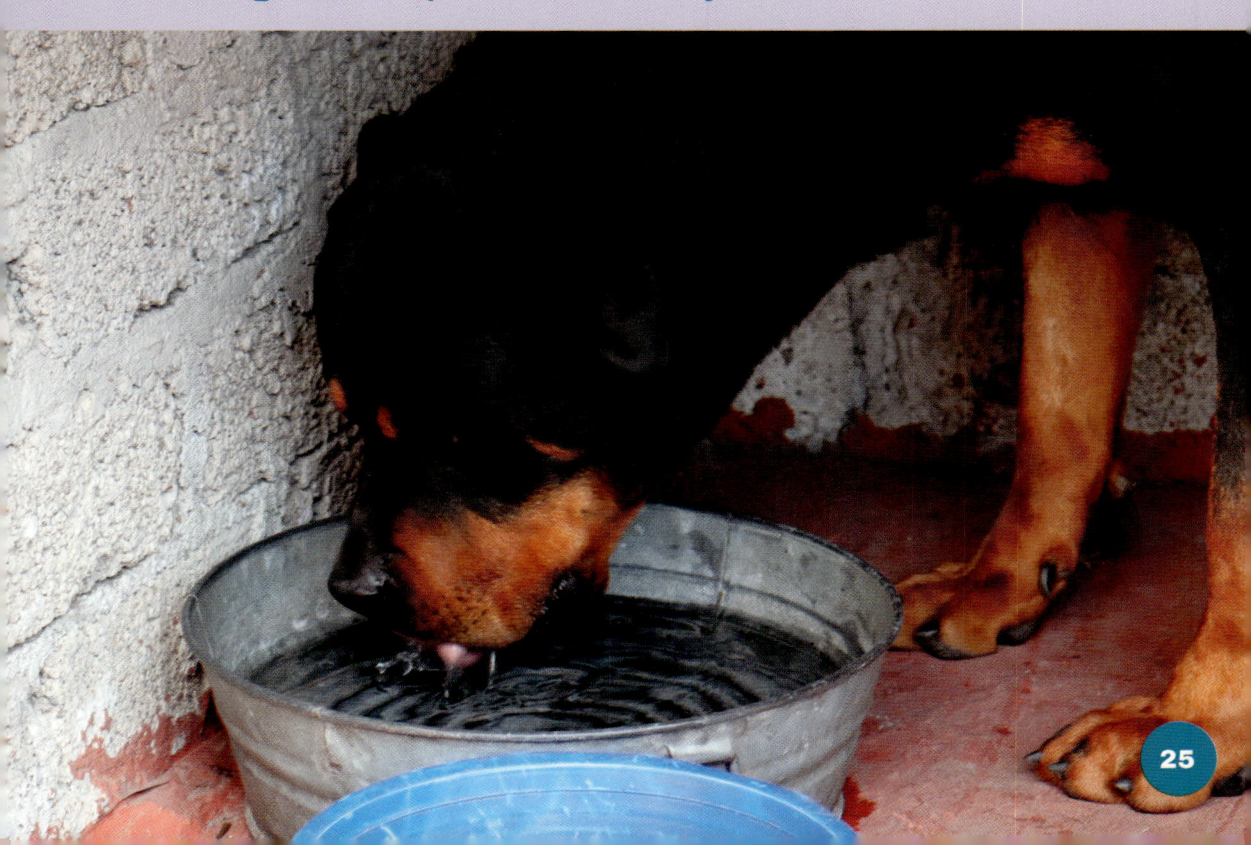

Training is also important. Rottweilers learn quickly. But they don't do well if left alone for more than a few hours. Owners should work with their dogs each day, starting when they are puppies.

Some places **ban** people from owning rottweilers. But the dogs are not born **aggressive**. Rottweilers can become mean if **neglected**. However, this is true for any breed.

Rottweilers may chew things if they are left alone for too long.

COMPREHENSION QUESTIONS

Write your answers on a separate piece of paper.

1. Write a few sentences explaining the main ideas of Chapter 2.

2. Would a rottweiler be a good pet for your family? Why or why not?

3. How much exercise does a rottweiler need each day?

    A. less than 27 minutes
    B. one to two hours
    C. more than three hours

4. Why should owners start training rottweilers when they are puppies?

    A. to keep dogs from forming bad habits
    B. because puppies never act badly
    C. because old dogs can't learn

5. What does **muscular** mean in this book?

*Rottweilers were bred to pull heavy carts. They are very **muscular**.*

A. strong
B. scared
C. lazy

6. What does **energetic** mean in this book?

*Rottweilers were bred to work, so they are **energetic**. They need exercise every day.*

A. slow
B. active
C. mean

Answer key on page 32.

GLOSSARY

aggressive
Strong and quick to attack.

ban
To not allow something.

breed
A specific type of dog that has its own look and abilities.

dock
To cut short or clip off.

drive
To move or herd animals, such as cows or sheep.

loyal
Loving and staying true to a person or thing.

neglected
Not given care or attention.

Roman Empire
A huge empire that ruled parts of Europe, Asia, and Africa. It lasted from 27 BCE to 476 CE.

threats
Things that are likely to cause danger or harm.

BOOKS

Barder, Gemma. *Be a Dog Expert*. New York: Crabtree Publishing Company, 2021.

Groskreutz, Rochelle, and Katie Gillespie. *Guard Dogs*. New York: AV2 by Weigl, 2020.

Oachs, Emily Rose. *Working Dogs*. Minneapolis: Bellwether Media, 2021.

ONLINE RESOURCES

Visit **www.apexeditions.com** to find links and resources related to this title.

ABOUT THE AUTHOR

Kimberly Ziemann lives in Nebraska with her husband and three daughters. She works as a reading teacher with elementary students. While she enjoys writing books for children, her favorite activity is reading. She also loves playing with her two dogs and snuggling with her cat.

INDEX

ANSWER KEY:
1. Answers will vary; 2. Answers will vary; 3. B; 4. A; 5. A; 6. B